M000282671

Library of Congress
Cataloging-in-Publication Data

Hanson, Warren.
  Dear Me / written and illustrated by Warren Hanson.
     p. cm.
  ISBN 978-0-931674-62-4
  I. Title.
  PS3558.A54378D43 2011
  813'.54–dc22

                                        2011010526

                    TRISTAN PUBLISHING, INC.
                    2355 Louisiana Avenue North
                    Golden Valley, MN 55427

                  Copyright © 2011, Warren Hanson
                        All Rights Reserved
                      ISBN 978-0-931674-62-4
                        Printed in Canada
                          First Printing

                        Please visit us at:
                     www.tristanpublishing.com
                       books with a message

Dear Me

Life Shared in Letters
between the Younger You
and the Older You

written and illustrated by

Warren Hanson

TRISTAN PUBLISHING
MINNEAPOLIS

Monday, July 27

Dear
I
rem   you will
                   m you, when
                      suppose
                        mean,

me
be li
ahead. So
write to you
find out.
    I hope this will
you somehow. I don't kno
where you live, or how old you
are, or even if you're still

FOREWORD

The lovely book in your hands is a time machine of sorts. Through Warren Hanson's elegant words and his wonderfully creative approach to issues of the heart, you will be transported, at least in your mind, to meet yourself at several spots on the timeline of your life. You'll reflect on the younger person you were, on the older person you will one day be, and on the ways in which memories can combine with visions of the unknown to impact the person you are today.

The letters that follow are, in some ways, very simple. Still, it's hard not to be emotional reading them. All of us have our younger selves – and our older selves, too – deep inside of us. What a gift it would be to have a conversation with the person we were and the person we will become. In these pages, Warren Hanson has given us that gift.

Jeffrey Zaslow

Dear Me,

I wonder if you will remember me.
I am you, when you were younger. I
suppose this is a little crazy. I mean, here
I am, a twenty-something woman, writing
a letter to myself. But a very different self.
Or maybe not so different. I don't know yet.

There are some things going on in my
life (I met a new guy!) that make me
wonder what life will be like for me in the
years ahead. So I thought I would write to
you to see if I could find out.

I hope that somehow this letter will

reach you. I don't know where you live, or how old you are, or even if you're still alive. I sure hope so!

There are a million things I'd like to ask you. About your life and your career and your family and everything. Because, well, they will be **my** life and career and family someday. But I guess I shouldn't start asking questions until I know that you got this letter. So if you did, I really hope you will write back. I would **love** to hear from you.

Sincerely,
Me

Dear Me,

What a delightful surprise! Yes, I'm still alive.
I'm in my late middle-age (or is it early old-age?),
and of course I remember you. In fact, it seems
like only yesterday that I **was** you. How nice to
hear from you after all these years.

Yes, I suppose you do have a lot of questions.
And I can probably answer most of them. I do
wonder, though, whether I should. If I tell you
things you want to know at your age, will it affect
the decisions you make in your life? And will that
change the life I have now? I don't know.

I do know that I'm very pleased to hear from

you. It's good to be reminded that I was young once. And maybe, if I can let you see what it's like at this stage of your life, I can help to assure you that being older can be pretty nice, too.

I look forward to hearing from you again.

Sincerely,

Me

Dear Me,

I was so excited to get your letter! I had no idea if mine would find you or not. It's good to know that you're still around!

I suppose it was a little strange for you to hear from me. And it was kind of weird for me to hear from you, too. Nice. But weird. I looked at your handwriting and tried to understand that my own hand would be writing that letter many years from now. Very weird.

Oh, I have so many questions to ask you, I don't even know where to start. I guess the first thing I want to know is, are you happy? Is your health okay? Do you have a good family and enough money? I really hope so.

I'm sure you've learned things along the way that would be good for me to hear. And of course I'm pretty curious to know what is ahead for me. I'm not too sure I really want to know. I kind of do and kind of don't. And even if I did, I wonder if it would change anything.

For now, though, I'm just glad to know that you are out there somewhere. I look forward to getting to know you better.

> *Sincerely,*
> *Me*

Dear Me,

And I am looking forward to getting to know you again. It's been such a long time. Did I really once have your youthful energy? It makes me seem so tired now.

I've thought a lot about you since your first letter arrived. At my age, I have a lot of time for thinking. You have brought back many smiles, as I've remembered so many of the wonderful times — times that you still have to look forward to. But I've also gotten misty-eyed a few times, thinking of all that's now gone, that will never come back again.

But maybe I can have some of those good times
back again through you. I look forward to that. If I
can help you as you look ahead, and you can help
me to look back, it seems like that could be good
for both of us.

Sincerely,

Me

Dear Me,

I'd love to help you with the good memories! Like, just last night I was with a group of close friends. Shawna, Ronnie, Rebecca, Jeff — that group. We laughed and talked for hours. Everyone brought food to share. We do it every year. We call it the Big Birthday, remember? Because several of us have birthdays close together. One of the birthday gifts was this funny hat that got passed around for everyone to wear. Remember?

After the party, on the way home, I wondered if any of those good friends are still in your life. I hope so. I think a lot of older people spend a lot of time alone, and I don't think that's good. Yes, like you said, it gives them time to think. But it can also make their world pretty small, and they can think about themselves too much. So I hope you still have good friends in your life.

Sincerely,

Me

Dear Me,

I don't think my world has gotten too small. If anything, it feels too big sometimes. And as for thinking too much about myself, I seem to recall that you were very much the center of the world at your age. So let's call it even.

Yes, I do remember that night! I don't think I've ever laughed as hard as we did about that silly hat. Yes, that was a wonderful group of friends. And I would encourage you to cherish those people while you have the chance. Those friendships are a treasure, and they won't last forever.

Some of those friends are still in my life. Several have moved, but we stay in touch and see each other when we can. In fact, we still celebrate the Big Birthday. It's just not as big now. I've also met new friends along the way, and I enjoy doing things with them. We don't often put on silly hats (well, in fact, never), but we have a good time.

I don't know if you want to hear this, but a few of those friends from that night are gone now. One of them left us when I was not much older than you are now. So reading your letter made me smile, but it also made me sad. I miss them.

There is one more thing I'd like you to know about that night. I still have that hat!

Sincerely,

Me

Dear Me,

Oh, I wish you hadn't told me that I'll be losing one of my friends soon. Now it's all I can think about. I can't help wondering who it will be and how it will happen. But I guess I should try not to think about that.

Instead, I will try to treat all my friends — in fact, everybody — like our time on this earth is limited. Like each time we are together might be the last. Because it really might be, right?

I remember the boy in my 3rd grade class who died so suddenly that winter. His desk sat there empty the whole rest of the year. It was so sad — and kind of spooky.

I haven't really had to deal with death since then.

Nobody very close anyway. But I know it will happen sooner or later. I just don't want to think about it.

Sincerely,

Me

Dear Me,

I still remember that boy in the 3rd grade. And his empty desk. His absence was such a presence in that classroom the rest of the year. But as you get older, your life will have more and more empty desks in it.

Two deaths that are ahead for you are Mom and Dad. Oh, don't worry. You've still got some time with them. But you surely know that they will not live forever, so I would encourage you to make the most of the time they have. Once they're gone, they will leave two very big holes inside you. Bigger than you probably realize now.

I finally made peace with Dad. You know what I'm talking about. Right now you don't know what to do about it, and neither does he. But you will. And so will he. The last few years you have with him will be the best the two of you will ever have. Too bad it had to take so long.

I was there in the room when Mom died. The

two feelings of sadness and release that I felt —
well, I don't think I can explain it. But I can say that,
when it happened, I was ready. And so was she.
For so many of the other losses, I wasn't.

Death is part of life. That's what everyone says.
But at my age, it's not just something everyone says.
It's the truth. I guess seeing our friends and loved
ones die is a way of getting us ready when our own
time comes.

But I'm not gone yet! So please don't stop writing!

Sincerely,
Me

Dear Me,

*I'm **really** glad you're still around! I hope you are taking care of yourself, so you will live a good, long life. So I guess I should ask — how is your health? I suppose you have some aches and pains, but I hope you're not suffering from anything serious. I could probably be taking better care of myself now, so that I'm in better shape when I get to be your age. I know I have some bad habits. But, you know, life is so busy. It's hard to find time to exercise. And healthy eating, well, just isn't much fun.*

I hope you don't talk too much about your physical problems, your pills and your doctors. It's just not interesting to other people, and it could make you seem, well, like such an old person.

I hope you have other interests to talk about —
books or music or world events. I don't have time
for those things myself, of course, but I assume your
life is simpler, and you have a lot more time on
your hands.

Please take care of yourself. I want to be around
for a good, long time!

Sincerely,

Me

Dear Me,

Seem like an old person? I **am** an old person! But I'm still kicking. Just not as high as I used to.

I do have aches and pains that I didn't used to have. I don't see as well or hear as well. (Maybe you should turn that music down!) Some of that is to be expected. And I've had a serious scare or two. You're right that if you were taking better care of yourself, I might be in better shape than I am. You think that you're going to live forever, and that there's plenty of time to kick those bad habits, and to start exercising and eating right. But believe me, that time goes by quickly.

And, yes, I suppose I talk about my pills and doctor appointments too much. My friends do, too. It's a pretty big part of our lives.

Still, you're right. I don't want to be a complainer. I don't want to talk only about myself, so that I forget to ask other people about their lives. I don't want people to run the other way when they see me coming!

So let's make a deal. You start taking better care of yourself, and I'll start having more interesting things to talk about than my own medical problems. Okay?

Sincerely,
Me

Dear Me,

I just got back from the grocery store. There was an older couple ahead of me at the checkout, and as I watched them, I found myself thinking of you.

The woman was mad because milk was so expensive. She was complaining to the clerk, who of course had no control over the price of milk. And the man kept talking to me and showing me pictures of his grandchildren and his dog. I tried to be nice, but, really, I just wanted to pay for my few groceries and get on with my busy day. That couple didn't seem to have any idea that they were holding up the line.

I hope you haven't become like that. I hope your world is not so small that you forget that there are other people, and that those people might have lives and schedules and worries of their own.

I do hope to have grandchildren someday, and I know I'll be proud of them. But I hope I'll realize that the strangers I meet at the store probably aren't as interested in my grandchildren or my dog as I am. I hope you will write back and tell me you haven't turned out that way.

Sincerely,

Me

Dear Me,

Your letter about the grocery store gave me food for thought. (Sorry for the bad pun!) It caused me to look at myself and ask some uncomfortable questions.

Yes, I am proud of my grandchildren. (That's right! You're a grandparent!) And I love to brag about their accomplishments. You will know what I mean when you get a few years older. And I do love my little dog. She is a wonderful friend and companion. But I really don't think I'm the kind of person who imposes my grandkids or my pet on others. Well, not very often.

You do need to understand, though, that when you get older, your world will get smaller. It doesn't happen because you want it to. It just happens. You start to slow down, but the world seems to speed up. The technology that is supposed to make things easier is harder and harder to understand. Everyone seems so busy and in a hurry. And, yes, everything costs more for me than it does for you. All of that can be kind of scary. So you take comfort in simple things, like grandchildren and dogs. You will want to talk to strangers, because there are fewer and fewer people to talk to otherwise. You won't want to drive as much, especially at night. So, yes, your world will get smaller. And it will happen without you noticing.

So I promise not to show pictures of your grandchildren to strangers, if you promise to be more patient with older people who want to show you pictures of theirs.

Sincerely,
Me

Dear Me,

Really? I have grandchildren? Oh, my gosh! Right now it's hard for me to imagine even having kids, much less grown-up kids with families of their own. But you must know all about that. You've seen my kids get born and grow up and move out. You've seen their joys and sorrows, their birthday parties and bad report cards, their first dates and their fender benders. You've heard them say everything from "Da da" to "I didn't do it!" to "I do." And now you've even watched my kids have kids of their own. I just can't imagine.

The other day I saw a car with a sticker that said, "Ask me about my grandchildren." I'll be glad to be a grandparent someday. But please don't tell me I'll have one of those stickers on my car!

Sincerely,
Me

Dear Me,

Oh, you will **love** being a grandparent. I always thought that being a parent was the best job in the whole world. Not the easiest, of course. There were headaches and heartaches and arguments along with the joy and the pride. And much of the time I was too busy with other things to do a great job of being a parent. But I did my best, and I wouldn't trade it for anything in the world.

But being a grandparent? That's even better! All of the fun without all the problems. Well, at least not as many. I can play with toys and read books and make faces and tickle tummies, and when I get tired, I just hand the little bundle back to Mommy or Daddy. It's so nice not to be so busy, and to give these little ones the time and attention they deserve.

I'm very proud of my grandkids. But, no, I don't have one of those stickers on my car. (Only because I just got a new car. The sticker goes on tomorrow!)

Sincerely,
Me

Dear Me,

I'm sick today. Some kind of flu bug. I was up several times during the night, and this morning I feel really awful.

It's not good timing. I'm supposed to have a job interview this afternoon. I suppose it's possible that I might feel good enough to go. But I doubt it. And I sure won't be at my best. I guess I should call them and tell them. It won't make a very good impression.

Remember when I was little and got sick? I got to stay in bed all day, and Mom always made a "surprise box" for me. It was never much of a surprise, but it was fun to get. There was usually a new coloring book and a cheap little toy. And she'd bring something fizzy to drink to help my tummy feel better. I could have used that last night!

I feel too terrible to write any more right now. I hope you're feeling better than I am.

> *Sincerely,*
> *Me*

Dear Me,

I'm really sorry you're sick. That's no fun at any age. I know I'm not your mom (even though I'm old enough to be), but I would love to take care of you today and help you feel better. I could put together a "surprise box" for you. I wonder what I'd put in it. One of those gossipy girl magazines that I remember liking so much. Maybe some new makeup. (I wonder if I could pick out what you'd like.) Oh, and chocolate! Enough for both of us to share! And if that didn't sound very good to you... there would be more for me!

I do hope you feel better by the time you get this letter. And don't worry about missing that job interview. As I remember, it all worked out for the best.

Sincerely,
Me

Birthday
Wishes
For
Someone
Very Close
To Me

Though you know
I can't be with you
As you celebrate this day,
We both know we are together
In a very special way.
So, although we're not together
As the years keep us apart,
On this birthday, and forever,
We will share each other's heart.

Happy Birthday

And many, many more!

Sincerely,

Me

Dear Me,

*Mom and Dad sent me some money for my birthday, so I felt like I could splurge on something nice for myself. I've had my eye on a cute little jacket at Panache (ooh, I **love** that store!), so I went right out and bought it. Luckily, it was still there.*

*It's a rich red, buttery soft lambskin, short and nipped in at the waist. Simple, but very sophisticated. It feels, fits, and looks great on me. (Well, I think so anyway!) I can hardly wait for just the right occasion to wear it the first time. My friends will be **so** jealous!*

*It's fun to be able to tell you about things like this. I wish I could send you a picture. But maybe you have one somewhere of yourself wearing this jacket. I hope you remember how it made you feel. It's **so** beautiful!*

> *Sincerely,*
> *Me*

Dear Me,

I loved that jacket! It makes me smile to remember how it made me feel to have it on. Like an Italian movie star! And I remember the first time I wore it. Some of the girls I went to high school with were going to get together for a kind of reunion. One of their families belonged to a fancy country club. I'll never forget walking in the front door of that clubhouse with that gorgeous jacket on. It felt like all conversation stopped and every head turned and every eye was on me. It was wonderful!

I don't look as good in my clothes now as I did back then. The years (and the pounds!) have taken their toll. I have to lie to myself a little when I'm trying to look nice. But even though I don't look the same as I did at your age, when I get dressed to go out and look in the mirror, I see a little hint of you looking back. And it helps.

In a few years, when you decide it's time to get rid of that beautiful jacket, you'll offer it to your cousin Chris, who will be quite grown up by then. And she will be **thrilled** to get it. The two of you will become quite close after that. She is still one of my dearest friends.

That jacket was expensive (like everything at Panache). But it was one of the best investments I've ever made.

Sincerely,
Me

Dear Me,

Mom and Dad are coming to visit this weekend, and I'm trying to prepare myself. I love them both dearly, but their visits — well, you remember.

My place is never clean enough for Mom. Dad thinks I don't take good enough care of my car. They're both good about pitching in and helping, but it's pretty clear that they don't approve of how I live.

I'm an adult. But I feel like a kid again whenever they're around. I want them to be proud of me and the direction I'm taking my life. It feels like I'm still seeking their approval.

But I'm really glad they're coming. I got tickets to a concert I think they'll like. And they both enjoy chatting with my neighbors. After a few days, they'll get back into the Buick and go back home. Mom

will cry, and Dad will be impatient to hit the road.
I'll watch them drive away with a mixture of
sadness and relief.

And the whole time they're here, I'll be thinking
about you, wondering how you feel about those
visits from Mom and Dad now.

                              Sincerely,
                              Me

Dear Me,

I know exactly what you're talking about. Even as the years went by and I got older and more settled, a visit from Mom and Dad always made me feel like a little kid again. It wasn't always because of what they did or said, really, though they could both be a little critical, especially as they got older.

But I would give anything to have them visit me now. To look out the window and see Dad easing the Buick up to the curb out in front. To help them carry their old suitcases in and get them settled in the spare bedroom. Even though I don't live where you live anymore, I'd still have to move boxes and piles of books out of the way to give them room, just like you will. I haven't gotten much tidier as I've gotten older.

I wonder if my kids — your kids — feel the same way when they see my car pull up in front of the house. Next time I visit, I'll try to remember to behave myself and not make critical comments about the house or the kids or the food. I want my kids to be glad I come to visit.

Good luck during Mom and Dad's stay. I know it can be a trial. But when you get to be my age, you would give anything to have them come and visit one more time.

Sincerely,
Me

Dear Me,

I just had to sit down and write to you to blow off some steam. That guy at work — I'm sure you remember, the one who always drives me so crazy — he did something today that was **so stupid**, *but he made it seem like it was all my fault. When I tried to talk to him about it, he told me to do my job and get over it. I ended up yelling at him out in the hall where everyone could hear. Afterward, I was angry with myself for getting so mad at him. But I just couldn't help it. He is such a jerk!*

Do you remember that? You must have learned a thing or two in all the years you've lived. Is there anything you can tell me to help me deal with these things better? I'm still so mad about it I could scream.

Sincerely,
Me

Dear Me,

I might remember the guy you're talking about. Gary? Jerry? But I don't remember the incident. If you are looking for wisdom from me, maybe that's it. It seems like a big thing to you now, but it will get smaller and smaller. Oh, that won't be the last time you get angry. There are other incidents ahead when you will lose your temper. One in particular that will do permanent damage to an important friendship. I got really angry, and I regret it to this day.

But most of the things that upset you will one day seem trivial. You'll have a hard time even remembering them, and if you do, you'll wonder why you let them get to you.

So if you want advice from me, I'd say don't worry about other people and what they do or say or think. Let your own behavior speak for itself.

Always try to take the high road. The other people who really matter, who will respect you and stay with you for the rest of your life, will notice. And the rest of them — like the guy who made you so angry at work — by the time you reach my age, you won't even remember his name.

Sincerely,
Me

Dear Me,

I think I'm in love! Do you remember this feeling, and how wonderful it is? How confusing it is? How all-consuming it is? I can hardly think of anything else. If there is anyone in the world who would understand how I feel, it's you.

Please tell me that this feeling lasts forever. I would like to know that, even at your age, I will feel this giddiness, this happiness, this joy. I would like to know that it doesn't fade or get ordinary or lose its magic.

Magic! How can we keep it alive? How can we keep those stars sparkling year after year? Is there a secret?

I would like to think that this love is the one that can stay alive and vibrant and exciting for a lifetime. Why not?

Sincerely,
Me

Dear Me,

Oh, yes, I remember that feeling. It makes me smile to read about your excitement and your optimism. And I'm not going to ruin it for you. Love is a wonderful thing.

But love changes. That excitement and euphoria that you are feeling now will mature and mellow over the years. It's like a violin. Do the great violinists of the world play brand new instruments? No, they all want to play instruments that are old. That were lovingly crafted from carefully selected wood. The older the violin gets, the more the separate pieces of wood settle into each other and become one.

A violin is fragile. It needs to be handled carefully. But it also needs to be played. Soft and loud. Sweetly and with gusto. That's how it gets its richness and depth. A violin is alive, and needs to

be kept alive through continual attention and use.
Like love.

Yes, I do remember how you feel. And I would
love to tell you that the magic will last forever. What
I will tell you instead is that it can get even better.

Sincerely,
Me

Dear Me,

Thank you for your beautiful and honest letter about love. I liked how you compared it to a violin. But I thought I heard a note (sorry, my turn for a bad pun) that made me wonder...

At my age, I hope to have a loving relationship that will last the rest of my life. You know whether that will happen for me or not. So I need to ask — will it?

I want to believe that, as the two of us grow and change, we will grow and change together. That we will continue to meet each other's needs, even as those needs change over time. That somehow we will keep the magic alive, though it may not be the same magic we started with.

But I am also realistic. As I look around, I see lots of people whose love has gradually turned into routine, then boredom, then distance. Sometimes those people drift apart. Will that happen to me?

> *Sincerely,*
> *Me*

Dear Me,

I was afraid you might ask about this. And I'm not going to lie to you — you'll find out the truth eventually. Yes, it will happen to you. That love that is so exciting now will change. And you will have to decide what to do about it. It will be the most difficult thing you will ever go through.

But I did get through it. And the life and love I have now is good, even though getting here required work, pain, and patience.

Everything you want, or think you want, has a price. The love you have now can last a lifetime, but you have to be willing to pay for it. It is up to you to decide whether it will be worth the price. And you may not know that until you've already paid. People you care about may pay, too. But each of us has to make our own choices. Then we have to live with those choices and do all we can to make them turn out good.

I won't tell you how this turned out for me, for fear that it will affect the choices you make. But in love, if you find yourself giving more than you are receiving, or taking more than you are giving, pay attention. If you don't change something, then change just might happen to you. And that will double the price.

Sincerely,

Me

Dear Me,

Thank you for being so honest. I guess you're right, that if we want love, or anything else that's good in life, we have to be willing to pay.

Unfortunately, I've been having a little trouble with that lately. Paying, I mean. I see all these things I want, but I never have enough money. Maybe you can help. (Don't worry. I'm not asking for a handout. I don't know how that would even work!) You are in a place in life where you can look back and see how things will go for me financially.

Sometimes I wonder how other people do it. Car. Insurance. College. Rent. Taxes. Plus the expenses of just living day to day. It seems overwhelming sometimes, and the worrying keeps me awake at night.

*But you know how it all turns out. So I hope you can help me stop worrying. Are you retired? Are you rich?! Just kidding. But I hope you've been able to stop worrying about money. Please don't tell me that you're still paying off the debts I'm piling up now. I **really** won't be able to sleep at night if you tell me that!*

Sincerely,
Me

Dear Me,

No, I'm not rich. Not even close! But don't worry. Those debts finally got paid off, though there were new ones to take their place. So, no, I haven't stopped worrying about money. I have a rich, full life, and money surely isn't everything, but that worry never quite seems to go away.

But you're right, I am in a place where I can look back. And what I see are all the things I could have done differently. Things that could have made my life easier now. I could tell you what you should do, but I know you wouldn't listen. If you did, I'd be better off now, and maybe I finally could stop worrying.

Yes, I'm retired, and I guess I'm comfortable enough. I have food on the table and a roof over my head. And, as I think I told you (or did I? I can't remember), I did get a new car recently. But I had had the old one for so many years that the repair bills were costing me more than getting a new one. I get to travel a little. My kids (and yours) live far away, so I go to visit them as often as I can (or as often as I think they'll put up with me!).

So I have what I need, but not much more. And I still worry that the money I have saved may not last long enough.

You could help, you know. If you could save a little more, and not try to keep up with "other people", life would be easier for me now. You don't have any secrets from me, you know. I know how you spend your money!

But, really, I'm doing fine. As I look back, I can see that there were financial ups and downs. When times were good, I did nice things for my family, for myself, and for others. And you need to do those things, even though later you may wish you hadn't. When you get to my age, you'll know that everything evens out in the end and you'll be fine. But you will never stop worrying about it. Because I haven't.

Sincerely,
Me

Dear Me,

*I'm sorry it's taken me so long to write back this time. I've just been **so** busy. I started a new job this week. And next weekend I'm in Sasha's wedding, so that's taking a lot of time. I just don't have time to write very much right now. But I wanted you to know that I haven't forgotten about you. I wish I had the extra time that I'm sure you have.*
More later.

Me

Dear Me,

I only have a minute. Just want to say that I'm really glad about the new job. I know you'll like it. I remember Sasha's wedding. Beautiful. Just got back from a Women's Club luncheon. I was the speaker! Talked about the life and writing of Sylvia Plath. In way over my head! Now I have to change clothes and get to a Humane Society board meeting.

Oh, there's my ride! Thanks for the note.

Me

Dear Me,

I bought the prettiest set of bowls yesterday! They're hand-painted porcelain with real gold around the edge. I didn't really need any more dishes. But these are so pretty. And they reminded me of the ones Grandma used when we were at her house at Thanksgiving. I couldn't help thinking that these might become family heirlooms one day. They might get passed down to my grandchildren, who would have fond memories of me whenever they get them out at Thanksgiving time.

Of course, I don't really have anywhere to put them. I don't have much space in this apartment, and my cupboards and closets are already full. But I just couldn't resist.

So I'm curious. Do you still have these bowls? Have they been used the way I hoped? Are your grandchildren excited to use them when they come to visit? I hope so. They are **so** pretty!

Sincerely,
Me

Dear Me,

Oh, my. Didn't we just talk about how you spend your money?!

Yes, I think I remember those bowls. Were they blue? The last time I moved, I found a box in a cupboard with some nice blue bowls. I couldn't remember where they'd come from — if I'd bought them or gotten them as a gift. I don't think I'd ever used them, so I sold them at a garage sale.

I'm sorry to rain on your parade. But when you get to my age, you'll have so much stuff! You won't remember half of it. And a lot of it will never get used.

The grandchildren do love to come for special occasions. But the things they think are precious aren't the beautiful things. They're the things they have attached good memories to. An old beach towel with a funny picture on it. A stuffed dog with an eye missing that they sleep with when they're here. There's an old box of Dad's tools that they can't wait to open when they get here. But beautiful bowls? They don't care a whit!

You'll accumulate a lot of stuff in the years ahead. Nice stuff, some of it. But unless it has love attached to it, it's just stuff. So save your money. I don't get much from selling your beautiful old stuff at my garage sales!

Sincerely,

Me

Dear Me,

I hope you won't take this wrong, but, well, it's kind of annoying that you know everything about me, and I know almost nothing about you. I love those bowls. But you've already told me that I was dumb to get them. You know all of my friends and what will happen to them. You know where I live, and how messy I am. You know where I go and who I'm with and what I spend my money on. I feel like I don't have any privacy.

But I know almost nothing about you. It's like you're keeping all these secrets. I don't know where you live or the names of your kids or whether you're still married or what your job was. You're being really careful not to let me know too much

about you.

I do love getting your letters. But they also

make me mad. I just wish they didn't make me

feel like you are, I don't know, snooping on me.

Sincerely,

Me

Dear Me,

Snooping?! You're the one who wrote to me first, remember. Sometimes you can be pretty annoying yourself. You keep telling me that I shouldn't let my world get so small and shouldn't think only of myself. But you can act awfully selfish sometimes. Like the only person you really care about is yourself.

I wish I could tell you more about my life. You and I have such a unique friendship. We have so much in common. I'd love to tell you about my family and my career, and whether my dreams — your dreams — came true.

But, you see, I can't. If I told you all about my life, I would be telling you how your life will be. You wouldn't have any reason to make decisions for yourself — to choose your friends or your career or your spouse — because you could feel like all of those things were already decided for you. Like you have no choice.

But you **do** have choices! Hundreds of them. Important ones and trivial ones. You deserve to make whatever choices you want. And to make mistakes, too. Then to figure out what to do about them. That's how you learn and grow. That's how you gain wisdom. (Not that I'm so wise.) If I tell you too much about how your choices turn out, it could change the decisions you make. And that's not fair. To you or to me.

The life I have now is the result of the choices you will make in your life. And I like the choices you made. Most of them. It's a good life. Not perfect, but good. Let's leave it that way. Okay?

Sincerely,
Me

Dear Me,

I'm sorry about my last letter. You're right. I'm selfish sometimes. I want my life to turn out good, and I don't want to mess it up. But hearing from you is really precious to me, and I don't want to mess that up either. You're right — I have to make my own choices. I'll try to make good ones. For me and for you.

Tomorrow I'm going on vacation with that group of friends. You know, the Big Birthday bunch. I wonder if you remember this trip. We have all rented a lodge together up in the mountains. There are hiking trails and a lake with canoes. And the lodge has a big fireplace. It all sounds wonderful. And yet... well, I just hope it all goes okay.

It's a big group of people, and we'll be living very close together for almost a week. Some have kids and some don't. And I know that a couple of the spouses don't really get along with each other.

If you do remember this trip, I wish you could write back to tell me if it all turns out all right. Wait. I know what you're going to say. That partly depends on the choices I make!

Sincerely,

Me

Dear Me,

Oh, yes! I remember that trip **very** well. How could I forget?

I still have pictures from that vacation, and I dug them out when I got your letter. They are spread out in front of me as I write this. They sure bring back the memories.

That really was a beautiful spot. The lodge was great. The sunsets were gorgeous. And the weather cooperated nicely, except for one rainy afternoon and evening. But we lit a fire in that big fireplace and found some board games in a closet. We ended up laughing a lot and having a really good time. That rainstorm gave us some of the best memories of the whole week.

I seem to recall that everyone got along pretty well. Well, mostly. I think there was a little disagreement in the kitchen one morning. And there were a couple of problems among the kids. But at the end of the week, we were all still friends. I think those two spouses even ended up burying the hatchet.

I do need to tell you, though, that when you get back home, you will spend the next six weeks with a cast on your leg. Sorry!

Sincerely,
Me

Dear Me,

I just got back from that trip with the friends, and your letter was waiting for me. It's probably a good thing I didn't read it before I left. It was a great trip, but I am wearing that cast. Stupid log!

I really love getting your letters. I missed them while I was gone. I was a little nervous when I first wrote to you. I wasn't sure what to expect. Or whether I would even find you. Or, if I did, would you write back? I'm so grateful that you did.

Before we met, I was kind of afraid of getting old. Slowing down, losing my health, taking pills, losing friends. It all seemed so sad. But you have shown me that life can be good at any age. You help me so much. (You probably could have helped me avoid this cast!)

And I hope I am helping you, too. If you will keep telling me the things that you wish you'd done differently in your life, I'll do my best to make changes that will not only help me now, but will also make life better when I get to be your age.

So please let me know what I can do to make life better for us both. I love getting your letters.

Sincerely,

Me

Dear Me,

I love getting your letters, too. They always make me smile. I remember that youthful enthusiasm. That energy and optimism. That belief that I could change the world. I wish I could get a little of that back. But my life now is good, and I can't complain (although I guess I do sometimes).

But I don't think that I should tell you how to live your life. Or mine. I already know how it turns out. For me, it's in the past, and I can't, and shouldn't, try to change it.

I've tried to be helpful to you, as you have for me. And I've appreciated your honesty. But I did some thinking while you were away, and I think it's time for both of us to live our lives, without each other's help. On your own, you will make the very same mistakes that I made, the same good and bad decisions. You'll meet the same people. Make the same friends. Have the same family. And live exactly the same life that I now look back on. You will learn much more from living that life than you ever would from me telling you about it.

So I think this should be my last letter to you. You need to live your own life, in its own time, without knowing too much about what's ahead. And I need to live my own life, in its own time, without thinking too much about the past. I do enough of that already.

You and I will meet one day. Somewhere in middle age, you will be able to look back at where you are now, and you'll smile and shake your head, just as I do. Then you will turn around and look ahead, and you may be a little bit afraid. But don't worry. I'll be there to take your hand and lead you the rest of the way.

If I could leave you with one piece of advice, it would be this: Live each day with an open heart. Graciously accept what each new day gives you, and don't complain about what it doesn't. Understand that other people aren't perfect, and neither are you. Try to leave each day a little better than you found it. Do that, and when you get to my age, you'll be happy. Like I am.

Thank you very much for writing. It has been wonderful getting to know you. Again.

Sincerely,

Me

Dear Me,

Your letter made me sad, but I know you're right. I need to live the life that I have right now, without worrying so much about the future. And you need to live your life too, without dwelling on the past and what you could or should have done differently. But I want you to know that I have come to like you very much, and I will miss you.

You were kind enough to give me one final piece of advice. If I could do the same for you, it would be this: Live each day with an open heart. Graciously accept what each new day gives you, and don't compare it to yesterday. Understand that young people are trying to do their best in the world they've been given, just as you did. Try to leave each day a little better than you found it. Do that, and, no matter what your age, you'll be happy. Like I am.

Thank you for answering my letters. I look forward to becoming you.

Sincerely,

Me